A Beginning-to-Read Book

Where is Dear Dragon?

by Margaret Hillert

Illustrated by David Schimmell

NORWOOD HOUSE PRESS

DEAR CAREGIVER, The *Beginning-to-Read* series is a carefully written collection of classic readers you may remember from your own childhood. Each book features text comprised of common sight words to provide your child ample practice reading the words that appear most frequently in written text. The many additional details in the pictures enhance the story and offer the opportunity for you to help your child expand oral language and develop comprehension.

Begin by reading the story to your child, followed by letting him or her read familiar words and soon your child will be able to read the story independently. At each step of the way, be sure to praise your reader's efforts to build his or her confidence as an independent reader. Discuss the pictures and encourage your child to make connections between the story and his or her own life. At the end of the story, you will find reading activities and a word list that will help your child practice and strengthen beginning reading skills.

Above all, the most important part of the reading experience is to have fun and enjoy it!

Shannon Cannon

Shannon Cannon,
Literacy Consultant

Norwood House Press • P.O. Box 316598 • Chicago, Illinois 60631
For more information about Norwood House Press please visit our website at
www.norwoodhousepress.com or call 866-565-2900.

LIBRARY OF CONGRESS CATALOGING-IN-PUBLICATION DATA
    Hillert, Margaret.
     Where is dear dragon? / by Margaret Hillert ; illustrated by David Schimmell.
       p. cm. -- (A beginning-to-read book)
     Summary: "A boy looks in all types of places inside and out for his missing dragon"--
Provided by publisher.
     ISBN 978-1-59953-546-3 (library edition : alk. paper) -- ISBN 978-1-60357-412-9
(ebook) [1. Hide-and-seek--Fiction. 2. Dragons--Fiction.] I. Schimmell, David, ill. II. Title.
    PZ7.H558Whm 2012
    [E]--dc23
                 2012012630

Manufactured in the United States of America in North Mankato, Minnesota.
     219R—122012

Where are you, Dear Dragon?
Are you in this little red house?
Come out.
Come out.

No, you are not there.
Mother. Mother.
I cannot find Dear Dragon.
Where can he be?

I did not see him.
You will have to look for him.

Here I go.
Oh, oh.
I can look for Dragon in this big box.

Look here.
Here is my blue ball.

And here is a red bat.
And a yellow hat.
But— no Dear Dragon!

I can look in here, too.
Is Dragon in here?
I want that dragon.

No, no.
He is not in here.
Where can he be?

Now there is a spot.
I will look there.
Will I find him there?

No, no Dragon.

Out. Out.
Now I will go out to look for Dragon.

Are you out here now?
Did you come out here?
I want you.

Are you in here, Dragon?
Did you get into the car?
No, I guess not.

Did Mother find Dragon for me?
I will go and see.
I will go into the house and see.

No I did not see Dragon.

Oooohhh! Did you go down here?
Come up. Come up.

I cannot find Dragon.

Mother. Mother.
I cannot find Dragon.
Did you find him for me?

Come here now.
We have work to do.
You can make the bed.

Oh, Oh.
What is this?
What is in my bed?

YOU!
Here you are Dragon.
You are in my bed!

Now here you are with me.
And here I am with you.
What a funny, funny dear dragon.

READING REINFORCEMENT

The following activities support the findings of the National Reading Panel that determined the most effective components for reading instruction are: Phonemic Awareness, Phonics, Vocabulary, Fluency, and Text Comprehension.

Phonemic Awareness: The /w/ Sound

Sound Substitution: Say the words on the left to your child. Ask your child to repeat the word, changing the first sound to /w/:

talk = walk	me = we	pill = will	pay = way
mall = wall	cake = wake	save = wave	tag = wag
bear = wear	pin = win	dish = wish	poke = woke
nest = west	need = weed	paste = waste	bait = wait

Phonics: The letter Ww

1. Demonstrate how to form the letters **W** and **w** for your child.

2. Have your child practice writing **W** and **w** at least three times each.

3. Ask your child to point to the words in the book that start with the letter **w**.

4. Write down the following words and ask your child to circle the letter **w** in each word:

we	who	work	paw	with	cow	crawl
well	will	throw	what	walk	tower	low

Vocabulary: Story Words

1. Write the following words on sticky note paper and point to them as you read them to your child:

   house bat ball hat car bed

2. Mix the words up. Say each word in random order and ask your child to point to the correct word as you say it.

3. Mix the words up and ask your child to read as many as he or she can.

4. Ask your child to place the sticky notes on the correct page for each word that describes something in the story.

5. Say the following sentences aloud and ask your child to point to the word that is described:

- A _____ is where people live and has a roof. (house)
- Soccer is a sport played with a _____. (ball)
- You can wear a _____ on your head. (hat)
- A _____ has four wheels and an engine. (car)
- Baseball players use a _____ to hit homeruns. (bat)
- You sleep in a _____. (bed)

Fluency: Choral Reading

1. Reread the story with your child at least two more times while your child tracks the print by running a finger under the words as they are read. Ask your child to read the words he or she knows with you.

2. Reread the story aloud together. Be careful to read at a rate that your child can keep up with.

3. Repeat choral reading and allow your child to be the lead reader and ask him or her to change from a whisper to a loud voice while you follow along and change your voice.

Text Comprehension: Discussion Time

1. Ask your child to retell the sequence of events in the story.

2. To check comprehension, ask your child the following questions:

- Where were some places the boy looked for Dear Dragon?
- What did the boy find in his toy box?
- Where did the boy find Dear Dragon?
- How do you think the boy felt on page 28 when he found Dear Dragon?
- What was your favorite part of the story? Why?

WORD LIST

Where is Dear Dragon? uses the 64 words listed below.

This list can be used to practice reading the words that appear in the text. You may wish to write the words on index cards and use them to help your child build automatic word recognition. Regular practice with these words will enhance your child's fluency in reading connected text.

a	did	I	red	with
am	down	in		work
and	dragon	into	see	
are		is	spot	yellow
	find			
ball	for	little	that	
be	funny	look	the	
bed			there	
big	get	make	this	
blue	go	me	to	
box	guess	mother	too	
but		my		
	hat		up	
can	have	no		
cannot	he	not	want	
car	here	now	we	
come	him		what	
	house	oh	where	
dear		out	will	

ABOUT THE AUTHOR Margaret Hillert has written over 80 books for children who are just learning to read. Her books have been translated into many different languages and over a million children throughout the world have read her books. She first started writing poetry as a child and has continued to write for children and adults throughout her life. A first grade teacher for 34 years, Margaret is now retired from teaching and lives in Michigan where she likes to write, take walks in the morning, and care for her three cats.

Photograph by Glenna Washburn

ABOUT THE ADVISER Shannon Cannon contributed the activities pages that appear in this book. Shannon serves as a literacy consultant and provides staff development to help improve reading instruction. She is a frequent presenter at educational conferences and workshops. Prior to this she worked as an elementary school teacher and as president of a curriculum publishing company.